# ECCEDENTESIAST

## INSPIRED BY A GIRL'S UNTOLD STORY

PUNISWARY P.

Made with ♥ on the Notion Press Platform
www.notionpress.com

Dedicated to every girl who has an untold story that is meant to be taken only to the grave!

# Contents

# Contents

# Foreword

Eccedentesiast: a story that reveals the pain that is often hidden within a smile. This is common for most girls in this century. I believe it is tough for some to even say it out in words as to what they feel at times, and that's where I've decided to pen these thoughts into words. This story portrays a common girl who had invested her hope, trust, and pure love just to watch how everything turned upside down in just one moment. How does she cope with all the struggles, especially from the society that chose to give her only a cold shoulder?

As a fresh writer, I chose to write this story in order to create awareness of the extent to which a girl could go, just to hide certain things from society. Deep down, she could be encountering multiple pains, but she would stow them away just to give you a smile and make your day. In line with that point of view, I believe that, as a debutant author, this would be the right story to start with, as it may bring about a better perspective on how strong a girl could be.

# Preface

It isn't easy to skip the phase of meeting the soulmate of your life, but when you meet one and it comes along with unexpected circumstances, what do you do?

Most girls are prepared to suppress these kinds of realities within their hearts and to continue walking along with them. This book would serve as an untold story for them. Yes, you may try asking the girl around you if they have an untold story, and I'm pretty sure that they will definitely have at least one similar story like this.

This story depicts the similar, untold story of a girl.

E.C.C.E.D.E.N.T.E.S.I.A.S.T

# Acknowledgements

**Indebted to God!**
**Grateful to my parents - Dr Siva & Mrs Thanabakkiyam!**
**Thankful to my brother and sister-in-law - Dr Komil & Mrs Gayathiri!**
**Obligated to my bestmate - Mr Kishokderan!**
**Last but not the least...**
**Appreciative to all my friends and well wishers!**

# Prologue

It was as though a sparrow sitting on a round rock had embraced me to join its friendly glance, and I ended up being a little too engrossed with the approach.

I've realized that the sparrow that embraced me with its friendly glance on the first day had flown and pecked the sky by shaking the whole world—my own world. One single sparrow brought lots of happiness, relief, and hope to live and dream—just to turn everything upside down. I have found the sparrow, but I've indeed lost my direction. A burden of sorrow has been filling me up.

# CHAPTER ONE

Every young girl imagines her nuptials. They each have lovely visions of organizing their weddings according to their own preferences. A girl should have a wonderful wedding ceremony so that she can cherish the memory of two hearts joining at the aisle in front of their respective ties, in addition to flipping through their wedding albums years later. Wishing for such marriages in life is not unjust. Not much would be on my wish list if someone asked me to describe my ideal wedding. On that day, the very least I could hope for was to be completely satisfied with the man I was married to and to have the biggest smile.

Do you not believe that the consent of both the bride and the groom is required for every wedding to take place? Why, in the end, would a girl's ideal wedding involve happiness and a smile? Presumably because she may marry someone merely for the purpose of marriage, or, to put it another way, because society is starting to view her age more positively.

Just because I've achieved my silver jubilee year doesn't mean that I consider myself an older girl. Except for me, of course, most people don't see it that way. Sometimes I question if getting married is actually a must or if it's something you choose to do. It is already required of a woman that she arrange her marriage as soon as she turns 20; therefore, I don't think it is just a matter of choice.

Rather than being a positive commitment, marriage is now a requirement. Due to society's complete ignorance of whether or not the girls are enjoying happy marriages, forced marriages continue to exist. The goal of society is to marry off the girls at the "right age." Correct age by their own reckoning, I would say.

What type of fantasy wedding can I expect in this muddled state of society that only makes my life more aimless right now? As I mentioned earlier, the very least I could hope for is to be joyfully and wholeheartedly married to a man.

# CHAPTER TWO

Days went by! I chose to divert my mind with way more interesting plans than marriage. One of the routines that I was thoroughly involved in was a reunion party organized by my friends. It was a long and tough process to decide on a day for all of us to be available to get together. Finally, we had a clear schedule on the ninth day of the sixth month of the year. It was successful enough because of Giselle's birthday party.

While we were at the birthday party, laughing our hearts out by reminiscing about old memories together, the birthday girl approached to inform me that there were another bunch of her friends who were on their way to the party. I found it exciting, as the bigger the crowd, the merrier it would be. We were all going to paint the town red today! Since we were waiting for them, we delayed the cake-cutting session.

"Here you go; they are here," said the birthday girl, pointing at a group of people who were walking towards us from the entrance. They were a group of four boys. She approached them and introduced us to the boys.

"Where is Kyler?" she asked them. I realized that I was wrong. It was not four, but a group of five boys. It appeared that he was on a phone call outside and would be in soon. Giselle was extremely excited to know that Kyler had attended her birthday gathering. "Wow! At first, I thought he would not be able to make it somehow. I'm totally glad that he is here now. KYLER IS HERE!!! Let him take his time to come in. We can wait for him! I don't mind even if it's an hour later," she told them.

At once, I was curious to know, who is this Kyler? I mean, what made Giselle so excited about him attending this gathering specifically? She has never exactly said much to me about him, though. Thus, I was wondering who he could be. She came to us to request a little grace period to cut the birthday cake, as she was waiting for Kyler as well. Filled with curiosity, I instantly asked her, "Who is Kyler? Why are you getting excited about him? Do you really want to wait for him?" Through her stare, it was obvious that I should not have asked that. It was her birthday party, and she had all the rights to decide in whose presence the cake-cutting should be done.

At one point, I regretted asking her those questions, yet I started pondering that if her concern for his presence to cut the cake was so significant, then he should have prioritized this instead of being on a phone call outside for what seemed like an eternity! At the same time, I was wondering why I was creating my own bad perception of him without even getting to know him personally.

"Awww, Kyler, meeting you after months is amazing!! Thank you for making my day!" exclaimed the birthday girl as she ran excitedly towards him. I took a glance just to kill the curiosity. Kyler walked forth to the table as he carried a helmet in his hand.

"Oh, Lord Almighty! What did I just see?" whispered my heart. Kyler was a decent-looking guy with a stylish beard, wearing a long-sleeved gray T-shirt, approaching the crowd. He took the opportunity to mingle with my group of friends, and that was when he greeted me as well. The moment was so beautiful, and as I communicated with him, I was instantly forgetting the bad first impression he imprinted on me earlier. It was as though a sparrow sitting on a round rock had embraced me to join its friendly glance, and I ended up being a little too engrossed with the approach.

Slowly, I realized that I was not able to move away from his charms, be it his way of approaching others as well as his mannerisms for all those hours. The cake-cutting session was smooth, and we had lunch together too. It was just the first day that I met him, but he connected with me by maintaining eye contact while communicating. Let me just confess to myself that I truly made a mistake by judging someone without even knowing him personally. And now, I have changed my whole perspective on him. He is such an adorable guy!

"Hey wait, how can you decide a person's personality in just 4 hours?" questioned my heart. The fluttering butterflies in my stomach stopped immediately.

"Did you find yourself talking to him so much on your first meeting itself?" Giselle asked me personally. I felt so embarrassed and said, "Yes, I'm sorry for saying that about him earlier to you, even before knowing him!" "You don't need to be sorry; it's his magic! He is such a gentleman, to the point that everyone easily adores him! Some may have the wrong perception of him, but that only lasts until they know him personally. Later on, they will regret it. You are not alone in this; I was just like you at the initial stage before mingling with him. So, be grateful that you are able to meet such a person," she replied to me. That shook me, especially after knowing about the magic he had on many people. In other words, I could say that he was extremely good at positively impacting everyone he met.

# CHAPTER THREE

Being back home, I felt as if my heart was a little heavier—as if I had left something behind. "What was that?" I wondered. I recalled the moment that Kyler walked towards us and the things that we talked about. "Yes, definitely this! This is the reason why my heart is heavy!" I whispered to myself. Since we had exchanged phone numbers, I decided to text him. "Hey, how are you? It was nice knowing you! Is everything good?" I sent it to him. At the same exact moment, I received a message from him saying, "Hey, it was great meeting you!"

And my earlier message got delivered to him at that very second!

OMG, did we send messages to each other at the same time? I mean, did we think about each other at the same moment? I couldn't believe it. And then he replied, "Hey, did we text at the same time? Wow, I like this synchronization!" I smiled at the text because I loved this synchronization as well!

We continued to text each other more often to learn more about each other. I was on cloud nine just to be able to understand about him, his family, his current job, his friends, his past relationships, and so on. I was extremely grateful, as he was able to share so much about himself with someone he barely knew.

Days went by. We communicated a lot through text messages. In fact, we enjoyed every bit of that until I could declare him as the one and only texting buddy of mine. We felt the presence of each other while we were in texting mode. It had been a constant exchange of texts, and we were embracing more joy by doing that. I realized that I had never been this happy before his presence in my life. I discovered clarity in my life, especially in my own needs and worth, after getting closer to a soul like Kyler.

# CHAPTER FOUR

Many months later, we took our own initiative to go on a date without any of our mutual friends. According to him, it was a lunch meetup, but it was different for me—I called it a lunch date! Wow, how amazing could it be? Meeting and talking to him, watching his charms, having a meal with him, and having very long conversations just on the first date itself. We just had a regular meal of rice with roasted chicken, but it tasted so good just because of the person I was having it with. I enjoyed every bit of the day, especially the rainy weather that joined us on that day. How much more beautiful could the day be?

Yes, it was just so beautiful that I still choose to smile instantly whenever I recall the day. However, I could not share what I really felt with him, as I couldn't predict what his reaction would be to it.

Moreover, I developed a new habit to make my feelings and thoughts about Kyler for the past seven months even more abstract. It was about spilling my thoughts, guts, feelings, and everything into a diary. Not a book kind of diary, but I saved them all on my personal laptop. It was for me to view and re-read it alone, anytime later, and smile at it. It was a sacred platform where I didn't have to hold it all together.

"Is this just affection or pure love?" "Is this a mere friendship or complete adoration?" These are the thoughts that rekindled me while I was pouring out my thoughts into words. I am a person who remembers dates and moments on any special day, and I have stored every little detail of those days on my laptop, especially the moments I met and interacted with Kyler. I won't deny that it was pretty hard to put my thoughts and feelings into words. It's hard to get the words right. But I knew that anyhow, years later, all these could turn out to be beautiful things.

Maybe, when the right time comes, I shall allow Kyler to read it all in order to know how much happiness he has given to me, how much relief he has provided me with, how many positive changes he has instilled in my confidence, how much he meant to me, how excited I got whenever I was able to meet him, how much I missed him whenever we were not texting or meeting, how much I prioritized his text messages compared to others, how much I thought about him even during my busy hours, how starting and ending my day with his text messages was special, etc.

# CHAPTER FIVE

At last, it is the ninth day of the sixth month of the subsequent year! I've known Kyler for a full year now! With a tiny chocolate cake and a range of dishes, we celebrated this together. I came to the realization that this entire year was extremely valuable in learning about the incredible gem of a guy he is. Most importantly, he felt the same way about having me. Never once in the 365 days have I felt like he takes advantage of me. While we acknowledge that everyone of us has busy times with our families, friends, and careers, we don't want to take the danger that we may treat each other badly or rudely just because we are busy. Rather, we would communicate honestly about our hectic days so that we can both understand why we don't text one another

"Probably because only a year has passed! It is possible that he is merely acting the part to make me feel more impressed. Or maybe he has a lot more secret personas that I haven't been able to uncover yet. Alternatively, this is the true him—a beautiful person on the inside and out!" I pondered.

One day, Kyler became dissatisfied with my actions. He detested me greatly for the manner in which I used to be incredibly kind to anyone who chose to use me for their needs. He says we should only contribute very little to people who abuse us to suit their own wants. "Being kind does not mean that we have to say yes to everything," he used to tell me repeatedly. He also says, "Just because we say no doesn't mean we're being impolite to them." He found it offensive that some individuals enjoy criticizing me when all they receive from me is satisfaction for their expectations. In order to improve me, Kyler has made a lot of slow but steady attempts to shape me.

Since then, I've realized that I can tell him anything and everything because he is familiar with my upbringing and my surroundings. He realizes that the reason I am a total giver is because of the role models I've had since I was a young child—my parents, who are experts at giving without expecting anything in return. I sighed every time he gave me careful instruction, thinking about how fortunate I am to have such close supervision in my life—especially without feeling fatigued.

And now, if I decide to think back on my ideal wedding, I can state with certainty that my one and only wish for my wedding—if it involves Kyler—may come true. It would be my happiest day as his wife, so I would have the greatest smile in the crowd!

Is it incorrect for me to envision myself being married to Kyler?

Is he the same with everyone else or does he truly like me?

Am I among his chosen ones?

Does he genuinely feel love for me?

Does he consider me to be his friend or his life partner?

Is it really his intention to be with me forever, or is it merely to be my friend until he meets his true love?

To be quite honest, I don't know the answers to any of these concerns, and I lack the courage to tell him how confused I am because I don't want to be the one to ruin our wonderful connection. I can declare with confidence that there will never be another Kyler in my life or the opportunity to make a friendship like this one anywhere, no matter where I go or who I'm with.

Weeping over spilt milk is pointless. Similarly, once I've expressed my feelings, I should not sit and mourn over the broken link. I made the greatest choice for us both when I decided to keep my thoughts to myself until I had some reasonable courage—or, more likely, until I had better clarity about how I felt about him!

# CHAPTER SIX

"Hey, I'm throwing a party tonight for my friends. Do you mind accompanying me to the party?" Kyler asked me in a phone call. As we were extremely used to texting, it was rare for us to talk on the phone. But listening to his voice asking me to join his party was something I couldn't ignore. "Do your friends know me? It might be awkward to be there," I said. "All of them know you, dear! They are just excited to see you," he replied.

Wow, why were they excited to meet me? I started imagining that he would have told them that his one and only special one had been invited to the party, which was probably why his friends were looking forward to seeing me.

"Hey, are you on the line? Will you join the party?" He interfered with my imagination. "Yes, I don't mind joining you, but where will the party be? Where are we going?" "Hmm, I'll let you know the location later. Let me come and pick you up from your house!" he initiated, coming to my home. It was exciting imagining him meeting my parents for the first time! I said a huge yes for him to pick me up from home.

It was half past five. "Hi son, please come in!" said my dad as soon as he saw Kyler at the entrance. I've told my parents a lot of things about Kyler, and from the beginning, they have always had a great impression of him. As soon as they saw him, their impression got better! It was a beautiful sight to watch my dad and Kyler discussing the current economy and their respective careers. As my dad has more exposure and connections through his job and experience, he was able to suggest certain areas for Kyler to focus on in order to develop his career further.

"The tea is getting cold; you can have a sip while talking, boy!" said my mom, involving herself in their conversation. Kyler smiled at my mom and spoke to her as if he had known her for a long time. While witnessing this beautiful moment, I started visualizing how amazing it would be to have a family like this. By this, I mean how amazing it would be to have him as a part of my family—by letting him be my real partner in life. I could see that my parents were very comfortable communicating with Kyler. In fact, it did not feel like this was the first time they were meeting. I was glad the first meeting went smoothly.

"Uncle, can you allow your daughter to come along with me for a gathering? I am having a small one with my friends. Will that be okay, Aunty?" Kyler asked their permission. Without thinking much, they instantly allowed me. That was when I realized that my parents trusted Kyler. My parents were comfortable with me mingling with Kyler. As soon as we left home, Kyler was talking so much about my parents. I was stunned and extremely attracted to his perceptions about my parents, especially the way he respected them.

"I can feel the positive environment that you have grown up in just by observing your parents for two hours," Kyler said. "What did you see? I mean, what did you find out from my home environment?" I asked. He replied, "I'm able to see their cautiousness in everything that they do in order to make you happy! I guess it is very rare for them to think about themselves. They probably think about themselves for just one minute in every twenty-four hours." His reply shook me! Wow, within two hours, he had discovered a lot of things about my parents. He learned about my reality in such a short period of time!

"Don't worry! I will protect you just like your parents! I won't disappoint you!" he added.

OMG, did I hear that right? Did he just say that he would be there for me? Did he just say that there would not be any space for frustration for me through him? I got excited, but I just smiled at him.

We arrived at our destination.

# CHAPTER SEVEN

There was a group of his friends, both boys and girls, by the street! They were near a bar. I was nervous and shy while looking at them, waiting to welcome me there. We got out of our car. I was wrong; they were actually waiting to welcome Kyler there. They were celebrating his presence. I was wondering why his friends were doing this. They invited us into the bar. I saw a table reserved for all of us with a cake set up there, as well as balloons decorated around the table with the words "Congratulations, Kyler!" My heart jumped a little while looking at the preparations. Kyler smiled at me and said, "I have been offered a job as a geologist at the Royal Dutch Shell! The opportunity was given based on the explorations that I have conducted to secure the samples here."

It was marvelous news to hear tonight! The unexpected feeling of astonishment within me led me to shed tears. I immediately hugged him. He held me close as well. All of his friends applauded him for this awesome news! We celebrated throughout the night with cake, beers, liquors, and wine. The night was one of the craziest, and we danced till our feet hurt. For every drink that I had, I found him watching me! I remembered him saying that he would protect me no matter what. By having someone like Kyler by my side, I decided to have more drinks and get more drunk. While dancing, he looked into my eyes and said, "I am leaving for The Hague in two months' time."

Ouch! This was exactly what I was not ready to hear. I was extremely happy for him to be offered this huge opportunity, but I was not ready to be apart from him. It was not easy to stay far away from him! I decided to think about it later, but he initiated the conversation about this in the bar itself. What else could I have done when I was drunk? I looked at him and hugged him tightly. He was blurred for a moment. He held me tighter, too. The tight hug was extremely precious for me. Yes, it was more precious than platinum!!

"Hey Kyler, let's do this! Let's play a drinking game! If you lose, you will have to drink one whole beer tower," interrupted one of his friends, Keith. While looking at me, Kyler laughed at Keith's challenge. He asked me through his eyes if he should agree to the challenge. To me, it was not about the challenge. He can attempt any challenges that he prefers, but I just wanted him to win. Win in everything. I did not want to see him lose at any cost, at anything in his life, even if it was just a drinking game. I knew I was probably being selfish, but I just wanted everything to be the best for Kyler! I said yes to Kyler through my eyes as well.

The challenge started. All his other friends were busy with their own things. Some were dancing, some were drinking at different parts of the bar, some were trying to talk in the midst of the loud music, and some were struggling to open their eyes to stay wide awake. I was the only one watching the ongoing challenge between Keith and Kyler. After 30 minutes of playing, they came to the point of challenging each other on the number of glasses of beer that someone can drink in five minutes without throwing up. I could read Kyler's behavior. He did not want to give up, as he knew that his friends might end up teasing him, but based on his reactions, I could sense that he couldn't drink any more. That was when I realized that I needed to give Kyler a hand. Whenever Keith was turning around or not really being observant of what was going on, I took Kyler's glasses of beer and drank them up.

There were about six glasses that I had tried to drink up for Kyler. Finally, Kyler was the one who won the game by drinking 15 glasses in 5 minutes, while Keith was at his 10$^{th}$ glass during these minutes. Kyler gave me an intense look as soon as the challenge was over.

# CHAPTER EIGHT

On the following day, I heard the personalised bird chirping sound on my phone, indicating a message from Kyler. Yes, it was a customized message tone that I had set just for messages from Kyler. I was so used to the sound of the chirping birds to the extent that whenever I hear this tone on anyone else's phone, it instantly reminds me of Kyler.

Kyler had sent me, "Hey, are you okay? All good?" I replied to him, "Yes, I'm still in bed. Haha!" He called me as soon as he saw my message. He asked, "Why did you do that yesterday? I mean, it was just a challenge. You shouldn't have drunk my portion of the glass. I didn't mind losing." I smiled on the phone. I told Kyler, "Hey man, I wanted to see you win. I wonder why I can't see you losing even in small things. Even if you are meant to lose something, I will do my best to help lift you up at least a little, just like I did last night." He replied, "You are just so sweet. I don't know the real reason, but I just feel that you are not at all fake. This is the real you! If this is the real you, then I am just glad that I met a special soul like you in this life! I have never seen someone like you in all these years. Thank you for existing, dear."

Those words were so meaningful for me.

After a while, Giselle texted me to ask whether I was available for a phone conversation. And we ended up talking for over an hour. Conversations about life were the best with her. And I was talking to her about my life without including anything about Kyler. It was mostly about careers. "Then, what's up between you and Kyler?" Giselle started in the middle of the conversation. My brain dimmed for a second. I wonder how I should reply to her question. Should I reveal what the feeling within me is for Kyler? Or since there is no major development, is it better to settle down for now? It is probably because I might have hidden certain matters from her, but I have always been honest with all my closed ones. I would rather hide it instead of deceiving her with fake information.

"There is pretty much nothing between us. We tend to have some interesting or funny conversation between us. That's it, Giselle. Why do you ask about it?" I questioned her. She laughed on the phone and said, "I just felt like there was some exciting bonding between you two. That's why!" I was curious to know the reason why she said that. She continued, "It's just that there are many friends that Kyler has. He almost treats everyone equally. In your case, it could be that as well. He is someone who will not be into another person completely. I can't say how special you are to him, but he used to talk about you. There will be at least once he mentions you whenever we are on the phone! You are probably really special to him. Or he is stating something about you to me since he knows you from my birthday party. He knew you through me, to be precise. It could be anything."

Again, my brain dimmed—not for a second, but for a few! We hung up as soon as we finished our conversation.

It was a wake-up call for me! I was wondering who I was to him. Is he really treating me special, or do I find it special because nobody else has treated me that way before? The reality kept hitting me, especially when Giselle said Kyler is someone who treats everyone just the same. Probably, he is being this gentle and sweet to everyone else, which I fail to realize in 704 days of being with him. If yes, then why am I falling for him more each day??!! I should be doing something about this. Either I have to stop letting the feeling continue or I should let Kyler know about my heart, which is falling for him every day.

The sound of birds chirping appeared on my phone. “Hey, why are you so quiet today? Are you okay?” Kyler’s message popped out. I wondered if he was sending these kinds of text messages to everyone with whom he is close or if his concern and priority were only for me. I should not be selfish by not letting him send messages to his close ones, but at the same time, I should not assume that his actions are especially for me. That is not good for my mental health. Here, I was creating every kind of random hope and excitement until I could still feel the butterflies inside my stomach whenever I saw him. Those butterflies should not die just because of the false hopes that I’m creating within.

I replied to him, “Yes, I’m okay. But I would like to tell you something very important. I just hope that it doesn’t affect you or me at any cost. Most importantly, I just want to let you know that as soon as I say this, if you want to keep your distance from me, you can go ahead!”

Kyler hated suspense. He wanted to know about it quickly. However, I was not ready to reveal it at that moment. I was hooked up with some work where I couldn’t spare much time texting with him. Back-to-back meetings and pending tasks were on a streak line, so I got to be more focused on that first. I asked him to be patient, as I would let him know about it that night itself. He was not happy about it, yet he agreed to instill some patience in him.

# CHAPTER NINE

During the night, many mixed thoughts have been pressuring my mind and heart at the same time. Should I tell it out, or am I deciding in haste? Is this decision based on what Giselle said, or does my heart really want to say it to him? What if he says no to these feelings? What if he stopped being the same to me? What if he stopped talking to me? What if he really chose to be distant from me, as I told him this morning? While everything keeps turning negative in my brain, I choose to delay revealing the thoughts to Kyler. And in order to ignore reality, I just chose to go to bed earlier.

It was the 706th day of knowing Kyler. The morning was filled with a number of text messages from Kyler trying to wake me up from the night that I was fast asleep. It was just to break the suspense. I smiled at those text messages. Along with it, I felt bad for going to bed without letting him know about it. I felt guilty for keeping him waiting for me the whole night. I texted him as soon as I got up from my deep sleep.

Within a few minutes, I received his reply. "Finally, someone is awake! Can you tell me now, at least? What is it about?" I felt extremely bad to see him longing to know about it, yet I got to enter my working mode now. I replied to him, "Hey Kyler, it was not a big deal. I'm totally guilty now of keeping you waiting. I'm so sorry. I have to go to work now. Shall we text tonight? I hope I didn't disappoint you!" I'm pretty sure that he was disappointed, but his reply was as sweet as him. He asked me not to worry about anything and to get into working mode first. He even said that he didn't mind waiting to talk to me about it at night.

# CHAPTER TEN

During the night, he initiated the conversation at around 12 a.m. Knowing that it was the weekend and I would not be somnolent earlier, he chose to initiate the conversation at that hour. He knew that I might get better privacy after this hour by being on my phone throughout. “Hey, can we talk now? We shall text if you prefer that way. See which way is comfortable for you. I am at a bar with a friend, but please tell me today!” he said. Out of nowhere, there was a feeling within me that there was no tomorrow. I decided that I had to reveal it to him today, no matter what. The worst part of these circumstances would be to witness a gap between the two of us. I totally believed in what was meant to be, and it will definitely happen regardless. Choosing to open up about my feelings might be the right call.

“Kyler, actually, I didn’t know that I would be close with you, especially after having the wrong perception of you at the initial stage. "Why did you even enter my life?", the biggest question that I have no answer to. Thank you for existing! Probably two years with you is the least, but I guess I can confidently say that I’m one of your close ones. I think I am falling for you, Kyler! I’m sorry if it is wrong. I will stop it if you don’t like me!” My text for him has been sent. Nervous feelings kept hitting me badly.

I needed some oxygen around me.

It was too hard to wait for his text, especially after sending something extremely significant. I prayed so hard to get a reply from him, which could soothe my feelings better. I know I'm being selfish, but I don't want to lose Kyler in my life at any cost.

"Oh, okay, I didn't expect this message from you. I didn't know that this was the message that I had been longing for for a few days from you. Guess what? I really like you so much. I am highly fond of you, but, as I said earlier, I am not interested in any relationship commitments with anyone. It is because of my past experience that you already know. You are one of the greatest buddies in my life. I can't really think of anything more than this friendship between us. I truly apologize to you for being the main cause of creating this kind of hope and feelings within you! "I'M FEELING SO BAD FOR DOING THIS TO YOU!!" Kyler replied after a few minutes.

This was a reply that I didn't expect. Probably, my assumption throughout was the primary reason why I developed my feelings for him. According to me, it was not his fault. I was confused by his reply, but at the same time, I felt relieved, as his reply was not harsh at all. In fact, he was concerned about my feelings. "This is not your fault at all, Kyler! You don't need to be sorry. As I said earlier, if you don't like me, I will put up my best effort to halt my feelings for you! You don't need to worry about me. There wasn't anybody to whom I've been attached this much; maybe that is why I fell for you so easily. PLEASE HAVE SOME DISTANCE WITH ME IF YOU FEEL LIKE IT!" I replied.

"What do you mean by keeping distance? Are you trying to say that this is going to affect our beautiful friendship? You don't need to feel awkward about this. Just be calm; I'll always be the same for you. If you expect me to keep my distance from you, then I think I will be the worst person for betraying you and your friendship. You are the only stress reliever that I have, and if I am being distant with you, where should I lead my path? This is super unfair to you, and I am not willing enough to do this to you! God is watching, Mike. He will punish me severely if I am hurting such a gem of a soul like you." Kyler replied.

That was such a meaningful text. I realized that he chose to have my back, no matter what came between us. I mean, who does this, especially after confessing deeply hidden feelings? Every common boy will try to escape the circumstances by saying, "Just stop the feelings, and you need to move on," if they are not interested in you. Instead of getting such a reply, I get a truly special text message from him. While thinking about how lucky I am to have Kyler, another message from him popped up.

"Hey, I feel totally bad for keeping you in this situation. I was hoping not to hurt you in spite of everything, yet I did in the end. I could not forgive myself for playing you false. I feel like I have the most loving person on earth, to whom I could never say goodbye for petty things. I didn't mean that your feelings for me are petty; I do respect your feelings, but this should not come in between us and break us apart. Anyhow, if you still need some distance from me, I can stay away from you. It's your call!"

Another meaningful text message, especially when I saw him being entirely guilty while I was having feelings for him." Thank you for being this concerned about me, Kyler! As long as you don't misunderstand my feelings, I am totally fine to be the same with you without any distance. I don't mind if you don't accept me as your life partner, Kyler. Your words in your text messages were super meaningful, and I will cherish them forever. I will completely be your good buddy as well as your stress reliever till the end! Lots of hugs to you!

"Thank you! Hey, I just have to say that I won't be inconsiderate of your feelings for me. Instead of ignoring it totally, let me tell you that I still have three weeks before flying to The Hague. I need some time to consider your feelings. I don't mean that accepting you as my life partner will lead me to disappointments like my past experience. As far as you being my life partner, it will totally be my blessing. However, I am just concerned that I wouldn't be your right man because you deserve the best! My past experience taught me a lot, as the more I am involved in a relationship, the more I might have the tendency to hurt you. If you are really keen about your feelings over me, I can actually let you know my answer for it in two weeks—a week before flying. Is it okay?" Kyler replied.

As soon as I was preparing my mindset to be a responsible friend for him, this text message entirely changed my point of view. At one point, I felt like I had the whole world in my hands. Such a beautiful hope sparkled within me. I am totally grateful for that text message. And now, I can't wait for his answer to my feelings. "THANK YOU, KYLER! There is nothing much that I can say about your being this considerate! Thank you so much!" I replied.

# CHAPTER ELEVEN

It has been a complete week since Kyler perceived my feelings for him. Another view of this timeline was that I still had another week to expect his answer to my feelings. During the entire week, there were situations that made me feel weird while communicating with him through text messages as well as phone calls. It was an awkward feeling that is not possible to express in words. Although he made me feel comfortable through his replies to my feelings, I can't experience complete contentment. I was at the edge of my seat, anticipating that things would get better as soon as Kyler responded.

In the meantime, Kyler asked me out for a lunch date. It was surprising to see him initiating the meet-up, especially after knowing my feelings for him—pretty peculiarly, he was totally guilty about those feelings I had for him. Instantly, without much thinking, I agreed to be there for lunch. I made sure that there were not many workloads to be done after lunch hour so that I could extend the hours with Kyler. I started keeping my nose to the grindstone from half past eight in the morning to complete the work before lunch hour.

Lunch hour! The very first date after my confession to Kyler. While waiting outside the office for Kyler to pick me up, I was beating the dead horse intensely. Thoughts were random on how the day would be—if I should initiate the conversation about my feelings, if I should pretend as nothing happened between us, or if I should repeat the confession to show my sobriety on it. I wonder if I'll add more glitches between us.

"Hey, what are you wondering outside the office?" asked Kyler through the car's windscreen while honking. The usual butterflies in my stomach increased a bit. I got into the car instantly. As usual, it was a difficult discussion to decide where to get our lunch. In the end, it was Kyler's choice. It was always this way because I am not good at making proper decisions. I would feel that the other party may force themselves to eat at my choice of location. We ordered our meal, and we were being normal to each other as there were no battles going on between us.

"Well, we shouldn't be this ignorant, especially after I am aware of what's in your heart!" Kyler said this in the middle of our lunch. That was really awkward. I was not comfortable looking at him as soon as he said that. I was just able to say one thing: "I'm sorry, Kyler!"

"You shouldn't apologize for revealing your feelings at any time. That's your rights!" Kyler replied.

"Looks like there are around 5 days left!" I reminded Kyler embarrassingly. He smiled at me and asked, "What if I told you that the timeline was just to make you feel better last week?" My heart stopped for a second. His timeline was my only hope that he might accept me as his life partner. If it was only intended to make me feel better last week, then it will totally shatter me intensely. I sat quietly.

"Hey, I was just kidding. Don't worry! I'm seriously considering your feelings. Or else, I wouldn't have invited you over for lunch. Just be yourself today while you are with me." Kyler said. Well, that statement completely activated my hope all over again.

"THANK YOU, KYLER!" whispered my heart.
I smiled at him.

# CHAPTER TWELVE

We were great buddies for the next five days. While having conversations with him throughout these days, my mind kept reminding me of how the day would be for us when Kyler reveals his answer. If it is a yes, it would be the greatest news of my life. As soon as he leaves for The Hague, there might be a long-distance relationship between us, which I don't mind at all. If it is a no, then I have to respect his decision and make sure the friendship between us is still strong. BUT, IT'S DEFINITELY NOT EASY!

"Can I ask you something?" Kyler asked me on the fourth day. I was curious enough to know what it was. And he approached me with a question: "Can I take like another few days to reveal what is running through my mind?" I was stunned. Probably he doesn't really like me, and he was trying to force himself to fall in love with me. That is super unfair to him. Am I causing lots of trouble for him? I replied, "Oh, sure, but I thought you were leaving for The Hague anytime soon. I just thought I would get the answer before you fly. If you are not interested, you can tell me, Kyler. You don't need to force yourself. I'm sorry for doing this to you!"

"Eh, what do you mean by I am not interested? You don't really know what's on my mind. I am just planning something small for you, which I would like to reveal once I'm there. That might be memorable and meaningful for us, maybe!" he replied.

That shook me. As he is planning to surprise me with something, isn't it a yes then? I was extremely excited. "Totally okay with it! Take your time, Kyler! I don't mind at all. I can wait." I told Kyler.

# CHAPTER THIRTEEN

Indeed, I wished to be one of those who were there at the airport to bid him farewell. However, I just thought that he might need some significant privacy with his family. Kyler called me. I picked up the call just to listen to his voice before he flew far away from me. That was pretty emotional. We were interacting on call for some time, and he was about to leave the place with a heavy heart.

Before ending the call, he said something so precious, "Please wait for my small plan that I have for you. We can FaceTime almost daily as soon as I arrive there! And most importantly, I really love you so much! Stay safe!" The statement from him made me to shed tears instantly. "I love you so much too, Kyler! Have a safe journey!" I replied, and I hung up.

My mind started to wonder about Kyler's departure, Kyler's arrival, Kyler's hostel, Kyler's tiny surprise for me, Kyler, Kyler, Kyler! Something was really wrong. I assumed that it was because Kyler was leaving far away. But that was not the answer. I can really sense something was wrong. Something bad was going to circulate, Kyler. Was it his workplace or the country? Something is going to impact him. But what is it?

I approached my mom. I told her that my heart was heavy, and she told me that it was because Kyler was leaving for a longer distance. Yes, she was right, but there were some bad instincts beyond that. I can't really explain that to her, so I chose to stay quiet. I started to pray hard. I prayed that no huge impact would affect Kyler at all. My random instincts kept hitting me. In order to avoid all of these, I chose to take a nap while waiting for Kyler to update me upon his arrival at The Hague. It would take more than ten hours for me to know about it.

Meanwhile, I received Giselle's call in the middle of my nap. It was quite weird—usually, she does not call me without asking if I'm available. I continued my sleep with a mental reminder to call her as soon as I'm up. However, I received another call from one of Kyler's friends too. That was pretty scary. I mean, what is wrong up to the point where a few of his friends are trying to reach me at the same hour?

I hope Kyler is fine! I attended the call and received a piece of news that shattered me completely. "Please check the flight name and so on; I just hope that was not the plane!" his friend told me. My hands started trembling. I switched on my phone data just to receive many text messages about Kyler. Almost everyone knew that I held his flight's itinerary.

THE HEADLINES OF THE NEWS WAS EVERYWHERE!

"Plane explosion before arriving at The Hague; injured three passengers terribly and killed the rest of them, including the crew."

I checked the flight name just to identify if that was the plane Kyler was on. Well, to be even more accurate, I was actually looking for news that could deny that it wasn't the plane that Kyler took. But there was no news that could deny it, which I could witness in the middle of being dreadful. My hands started quivering to scroll through each and every piece of news on the web pages that I've been checking. I refreshed those pages hundreds of times, expecting that I'd be reading some sort of horrible joke.

I started feeling as if my heart was breaking into pieces while looking at every piece of news that had no hope. My loud scream to my parents made them out of control as well.

"That sweet boy! He doesn't deserve this!" said my dad. That was the very first moment I noticed my dad shed tears. I realized how special Kyler was to him. My mom was in shock for such a long time. They started changing TV channels to find out further news about the plane. They were hoping for any news that could make things calmer, yet every hope that they had gone haywire till the end.

"Kyler, I hope you are okay! If loving me back is why you are facing this, then I am always ready to let you go. I just need you to be safe and sound! The earth needs you, Kyler!" I pondered. I did not have enough guts to join my parents in watching the news because, deep down, I still hoped Kyler would be one of the injured ones. DEFINITELY NOT DEAD! I was not ready to watch something unexpected on the news.

"Hey, how long should I wait for you? Please come fast!" Kyler said. "I'm getting ready now. I will be there in five minutes," I replied. Instantly, I opened my eyes, only to end up realizing that I had a short escape from reality to have Kyler in my dream. Tears rolled down my cheeks. All I could do was cry my heart out to know that the short dream would not become reality at all.

"I just hope Kyler is fine!" I murmured.

My mom knocked on the door and entered my room. She looked at me. I knew she would want to ask if I was okay, but since she knew the answer by looking at my face, she chose to stay silent. “Is there any update on Kyler?” I asked my mom. She said that it’s been the same update so far, and she hoped for Kyler to be safe.

Most of his and my friends approached me to check on me. If they knew his absence was impacting me, then they should know what kind of bond we were sharing. I wondered what Kyler had really shared about me with his friends.

# CHAPTER FOURTEEN

It has been a week of not getting official updates about the plane. Rumors were spreading everywhere about the plane. It was the toughest seven days for not being able to communicate with the only soul that I have never skipped talking to in these three years. I've been viewing my feeds about Kyler from his family and friends. Those posts shattered me totally.

I muttered, How would Kyler have faced the situation when his body turned weightless when the plane dived and exploded? What would his mindset have been when his body rose up from the seat and his limbs were floating while the objects around him hovered? I could not resist thinking about Kyler for the whole week. Tears all the time!

Most of them stood by my side as they understood my feelings, while some of them criticized that I don't need to pretend as if losing Kyler was affecting me big time because I knew him for about 1000 days only. I was not ready to explain to each and every one of them what kind of attachment we had in less time.

I was used to having Kyler in everything I did. He was my everything, and he will always be. I was not equipped to eloquently express my feelings. A forever of lessons and memories from the one and only Kyler.

All the sleepless nights and plain mornings that I walked into thereafter were to check for updates about the plane hopelessly. I failed tremendously in managing my tasks at work. I failed in everything I did. I felt as though there was no purpose to truly walk around, although I have my family waiting for me behind me.

In the past two weeks, I have started communicating with Kyler's family. I chose to be there for his family members, as I knew how much his family meant to him. I realized how lucky Kyler was to have such a precious family. I have been visiting them often just to let them know miracles do happen, and I will be there for them regardless.

Do miracles really happen? As I strongly believed that Kyler would be coming back to us, I could say that I do rely on miracles. I'm a strong believer that whoever is meant to be in your life will always gravitate back to you, no matter how far they wander!

BUT, IMPORTANTLY, THE PERSON SHOULD BE ALIVE!

Slowly, my family was not happy with my behavior. The changed behavior, to be even more precise, was existent just for the sake of it. They started showing me their frustration, as I was highly reluctant to do anything. Well, they observed me more than I do.

"The bodies from the plane explosion were burned and severely disfigured, as many were charred beyond recognition. DNA samples are being collected from respective family members to be sent to health officials for further identification. Three injured victims who bit the dust as well were sent for the post-mortems," official news revealed after seventeen days.

Was it expected news? Or was it another shattered moment? Although I was hoping for some miracles to happen, not to fabricate them, deep down I knew that Kyler would not be coming back to us. The news was sufficient to find out that every passenger and crew member were no more.

Kyler's family got completely drained after the news. The hope that they had while sending the DNA samples of Kyler was all enervated on the blink.

# CHAPTER FIFTEEN

Two days later, every relevant family was requested to be at the airport. Receiving someone's body in pieces via cargo planes would be the worst. It would only be sent upon request, and Kyler's family has requested it.

I was not prepared to see Kyler in that condition. I was probably selfish, but I was not confident in myself, so I might be broken there. I can't be an appropriate strength for the family. Thus, I decided not to go there.

Hours later, I received the information that Kyler's body was. Should I attend the funeral? Thoughts killed me continuously. I was totally not ready to witness Kyler in a coffin. My parents asked me if I wanted to remember the smiling face of Kyler or have the memory of his final day. After having a deep thought about it, I decided not to attend the funeral. Again, I took the decision in selfish mode. It should be a strength for his family and close ones if I choose to be there, not a burden.

I prayed for Kyler from my home. I wished that he would forgive me for my decision. I was trying to fix myself by the time the final rites were completed, but I failed. Anyhow, the funeral was conducted smoothly.

I received a phone call from Kyler's mother three days later. I was hesitant to speak to her because the pain that they were enduring was the biggest compared to mine; hence, I can't be sharing that I was unable to see him in a coffin for not attending the funeral. Yet, I've got her voice saying that she understood why I was not around during the funeral and that I could go to her house whenever I wanted to hereafter.

# CHAPTER SIXTEEN

Days went by while I was filling so much emptiness within myself. Waking up in the middle of the night to chase after Kyler and walking around the day to constantly find answers to my questions in Kyler's absence were my unremitting actions throughout.

The first man that I fall for will remain my secret and will be taken to the grave! The story ended even before it began.

I've realized that the sparrow that embraced me with its friendly glance on the first day has flown and pecked the sky by shaking the whole world—my own world. One single sparrow brought lots of happiness, relief, and hope to live and dream—just to turn everything upside down. I've lost the direction, indeed. The burden of sorrow has been filling me up! I chose to watch myself drown more in misery and depression.

As I was being a loner, I understood my life path further. I realized that this pain was much more meaningful. No matter how much time I chose to heal, I preferred to hold onto the pain of Kyler's absence, especially whenever I feel the pain is fading at times. I've realized that I have become way quieter than before. I wasn't sure if it was because of the broken experience I had from losing Kyler or if it was the life path that was made by my own choice. Anyhow, I've started loving myself for being this way.

More questions arose as the months passed.

Why was I not lucky enough to keep someone I love so much for so long? Why did Kyler come forward and become the biggest part of my life if all it was meant was for him to leave halfway? Where did Kyler's promises go? Why did he choose to be there for me and make me rely on it? Why was Kyler's plane not designed with a detachable cabin? Why couldn't I get Kyler's answer on my feelings a little earlier? How would I give Kyler the opportunity to read my daily thoughts that have been stored on my laptop? What will happen to my dream wedding? Will I ever be able to smile on my wedding aisle? Will I ever be able to find myself someone like Kyler? Will I ever be able to see Kyler in my lifetime?

# CHAPTER SEVENTEEN

"Move on!! He is not your lover!!"

"I don't understand what is wrong with you! Kyler is just a passing cloud in your life! Why are you spoiling your life for him?"

"Kyler is not your better half! Stop acting like he is! His family and friends are facing more pain than you!"

"You should not be facing life in this way for a person that you knew just for three years! You have life ahead of you!"

"I wonder why Kyler is playing a huge role in your life when he was just there for you as he was for anyone else!"

"Kyler's time is over! He has lived his life to the fullest! Don't waste your time on earth by thinking about him!

Those words have been hitting my ears for approximately twenty-four months from those who were not ready to be my shoulder. Those were the people who had Kyler as one of their close ones. As per me, Kyler was my one and only close one. I believed there was a mere difference between these two.

I've realized that many have started blaming Kyler for the changes I've encountered in my behavior. I can't definitely be the primary cause of Kyler's being blamed. Therefore, I have decided to stop doing this. Stopped showing the changes on the outside while sustaining them from within.

# CHAPTER EIGHTEEN

ECCEDENTESIAST.

I've learned to be an eccedentesiast. I've learned to smile at everyone around me and talk as much as I can - but with the existing pain without having it reduced to even minimal. I've understood how life should be shown to people who are not ready to listen to my rants. I've slowly become an expert in being eccedentesiast.

I've made sure that only my pillows and lavatory recognize the real me—nowhere else, nobody else.

And it finally made me be as I had been since Kyler left. There was no turning back to earlier times. In fact, I don't remember how my deportation was before Kyler left. Those were the days when I'd been laughing my heart out and being cheerful. And it turned out to be where I was not able to leave my bed or get into reality. At times, I preferred to continuously hug my pillows for the entire day, as it was the best buddy of mine as an eccedentesiast.

I've been a cold person. I've been vulnerable enough that I started fearing attachments. I don't want anybody to take my depression or sufferings as an advantage to get attached to me. I've been distant enough from everybody else, although I've had a few that were prepared to give me their touch of healing for my scars.

In the middle of the race of being someone's priority, I've started being my own.

# CHAPTER NINETEEN

It was habitual for me to have a random conversation with Kyler's family in order to check if things were fine with them. However, on one particular day, the call was for a different purpose.

"Do you have any idea what the plan is that Kyler has been planning for you?" asked his elder sister. The question quaked me, as my assumption that my love for Kyler has been kept in secrecy was wrong for all these years. Little did I know that he was sharing almost everything about me with his family. He has been saying loads of things about me and my feelings to his mother and sister.

It seemed that his mother and sister have been convincing him that not all the girls would be creating relationships like his past experience and that I would be the right partner for him. He has been completely considerate of my feelings because of their constant confidence in me.

His invitation to lunch after my love confession was his sister's idea to have the vibe of mingling as partners. Kyler's response after the lunch was so positive that he felt as if he found me not faking around and that he would be falling for me indefinitely. He has been adoring my creative ways of showing love and has started falling for me.

My heart was getting a lot more scars despite owning existing wounds deep down while hearing all these from her after years of relentless sobbing and wailing.

She continued, weeping, that he had planned a beautiful surprise for me so that I would find my love proposal worthy. It was a plan for him to decorate his room in The Hague with our picture moments together by specifying the dates. He has planned to FaceTime me as soon as the decoration is completed. He would want to show me his room, filled with the moments we shared for all those years, and propose to me accepting me as his life partner.

The surprise plan has moved me way too much. I missed his presence the most, like any other day, as soon as I listened to the story. That whole night was about thinking about how peaceful and happier my life would have been if Kyler was alive.

# CHAPTER TWENTY

Sometimes, home isn't four walls. It's an individual. Kyler is my home!

I have always been thankful for this birth of mine, as I was meant to meet a soul like Kyler in my lifetime.

"I would have been yours, Kyler! Anyhow, I am still yours! I love you, Kyler!" I mumbled from the time that I knew what was in Kyler's mind, to be exact.

Kyler needed me, as he trusted that I could be his right one. I should be playing my role as his partner. Eccedentesiast has taught me how to keep my life focused on only one person. None other than Kyler.

"How long do you choose to be like this? We are getting old. We would want to settle our responsibilities before we depart for good. Either you find someone yourself or we will start finding the right one for you," my parents said to me. They are not aware of my feelings for him, yet they guessed that Kyler could be one of the reasons that I am not moving forward.

Am I able to find another Mr. Right when my eyes and heart were only for Kyler? I knew that I was hurting them, but I was not willing enough to betray Kyler, who chose to be my life partner either.

I knew my dream wedding would not be achieved somehow; I knew I would not be smiling at my wedding aisle. I knew I would not be glad to marry someone else.

I knew I would spoil someone's life if I married just for the sake of getting it done. All I knew was that I could be peaceful and gratified if I lived with the memories of Kyler, especially after knowing Kyler had been looking forward to becoming mine too.

Being eccedentesiast has made me highly affectionate towards Kyler's family as well. I would have been a part of the family if Kyler and I had been together. Thus, I should be playing the role of a member of the family. I have contributed and devoted my best to the family, just as I am to my own family. They have accepted me as one of their family members and treated me as another Kyler.

"For not having Kyler physically, we are having you instead," said Kyler's parents to me. It was such a meaningful statement from them that I will cherish in my remaining days.

Probably I would not have earned these kinds of words and trust from them if I had put my pain and Kyler's absence aside. I probably would not have a proper attachment to Kyler's family if I had been ignorant about losing Kyler. I was totally grateful to myself for being a complete eccedentesiast. Let the world know that I am fine, but deep down, I have recognized the real me.

Instead of completely walking away from the shadow of Kyler, I'd rather be an eccedentesiast!

Thank you, Kyler, for coming to me!

Thank you, Kyler, for choosing me!

Thank you, Kyler, for being a huge part of my life!

Thank you, Kyler, for being there as my strength and comfort!

Thank you, Kyler, for being mine!

You will be forever tucked into my heart and life, Kyler!

I love you!

# Epilogue

I wish heartfelt good luck to each and every girl who has a similar kind of struggle in life. I wish lots of strength to endure and encounter this with lots of spirit and be an inspiration to many!

You go, girl!

www.ingramcontent.com/pod-product-compliance
Lightning Source LLC
La Vergne TN
LVHW040957150826
845672LV00002B/728

* 9 7 9 8 8 9 0 6 6 4 1 4 3 *